"He has risen!"
—Mark 16:6

ZONDERKIDZ

The Berenstain Bears® and the Easter Story

Copyright © 2012 by Berenstain Publishing, Inc.
Illustrations © 2012 by Berenstain Publishing, Inc.

Requests for information should be addressed to:

Zonderkidz, 3900 Sparks Dr. SE *Grand Rapids, Michigan 49546*

This Hobby Lobby edition ISBN: 978-0-310-63039-5

Editor: Mary Hassinger
Art direction: Cindy Davis

Printed in China

15 16 17 18 19 20 /DSC/ 15 14 13 12 11 10 9 8 7 6 5 4

The Berenstain Bears
and the
Easter Story

written by Jan & Mike Berenstain

ZONDERVAN.com/
AUTHORTRACKER
follow your favorite authors

Living
Lights™

ZONDERkidz

It was springtime in Bear Country, and Brother, Sister, and Honey Bear were thinking about Easter. Actually, they were thinking about Easter candy. They loved Easter candy—there were so many different kinds! They were even thinking about it on their way to Sunday school one fine spring morning.

"My favorite Easter candy is chocolate bunnies," said Brother.

"My favorite is marshmallow chicks," said Sister.

"Jelly beans!" cried Honey Bear.

Their Sunday school teacher, Missus Ursula, overheard them. "I like the black jelly beans best," she smiled. "But, you know, there's much more to Easter than chocolate bunnies, marshmallow chicks, and jelly beans—black or otherwise."

"Sure, we know that," said Brother.

"Sure," said Sister.

"Sure!" said Honey.

"Oh?" said Missus Ursula. "Then why don't you tell the class all about Easter?"

"Well," said Brother, scratching his head, "it's about stuff in the Bible."

"Yeah," agreed Sister. "Bible stuff."

"Stuff!" nodded Honey.

"Hmmm," said Missus Ursula. "Maybe it's time we learned a little more about this 'Bible stuff.' It happens that the cubs in the next class are about to put on a play called *The Easter Story*."

"Can we watch, Missus Ursula?" the cubs asked.

"Just what I was about to suggest," she said.

In the next classroom, everything was ready. Scenery was set up and the performers were in costume. One of them began to read the story out loud:

"Long ago, in the Holy Land, there was a man named Jesus. He traveled the countryside teaching about God and what God wanted for his people. Many listened to Jesus and followed him."

"Jesus was able to perform miracles. One time, he turned water into wine.

Another time he made a lame man walk. Jesus could do these wonderful things because he was the Son of God. He was called the Christ, which is a name for a king. But Jesus' kingdom is the kingdom of heaven."

"Jesus sometimes made people angry. Many people found his teachings strange, and some doubted that he was the Son of God. Others worried about why he was called 'king.' They were afraid that Jesus would become too powerful."

"Jesus was from a small country town. But he traveled all the way to the Holy City of Jerusalem. One day, as he rode into the Holy City on a donkey, crowds of people greeted him. They shouted, 'Hosanna!' which means 'Save us!' The leaders of the city grew worried. Was Jesus becoming too powerful?

"One night, Jesus went to a garden to pray. While he prayed, soldiers were sent to arrest him. They took him away to prison."

"Jesus was brought before a wicked judge. The judge asked Jesus many questions. He wanted to show everyone that Jesus was not a king. So he ordered Jesus to be put to death by hanging on a wooden cross."

"After Jesus died, his friends took him away. They put him in a tomb that was closed with a great stone.

Jesus was in the tomb for two days."

"On the morning of the third day after Jesus died, some women who knew Jesus came to weep at his tomb. They saw that the stone was rolled away and Jesus was gone. But an angel told the women not to be afraid. He told them that Jesus was alive once more."

"Jesus came to visit his friends after he rose. They were amazed and fell down and worshiped him. Jesus told them they should spread the good news about what had happened."

"Finally, Jesus rose up to heaven to be with God, his Father."

The play was over. Everyone was very quiet.

"Easter is about a lot more than candy, isn't it?" asked Sister.

"Yes, indeed," said Missus Ursula. "Are there any questions?"

"Yes," said Brother. "Does this mean we shouldn't eat any Easter candy?"

"Certainly not!" laughed Missus Ursula. "I wouldn't want to miss my black jelly beans either! It just means that on Easter morning, after you get your Easter baskets, you'll all go to church to learn more about Easter."

"Hooray!" the cubs said.

"And Hosanna!" added Missus Ursula. "He is risen!"

"Amen to that!" said Brother and Sister.